Let's Eat!

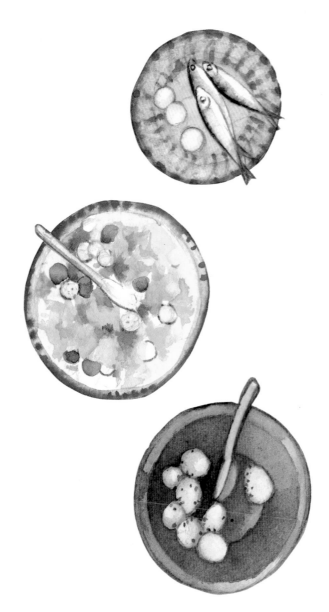

WRITTEN BY **Ana Zamorano**

ILLUSTRATED BY **Julie Vivas**

SCHOLASTIC INC.

New York Toronto London Auckland Sydney
Mexico City New Delhi Hong Kong

In my family there are seven of us.
Mamá, Papá, Granny and Grandpa,
my brother Salvador, my sister Alicia,
and me.

I am the smallest and Mamá
is the biggest. She is going to
have a baby any day now.

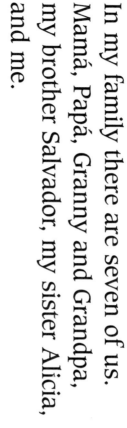

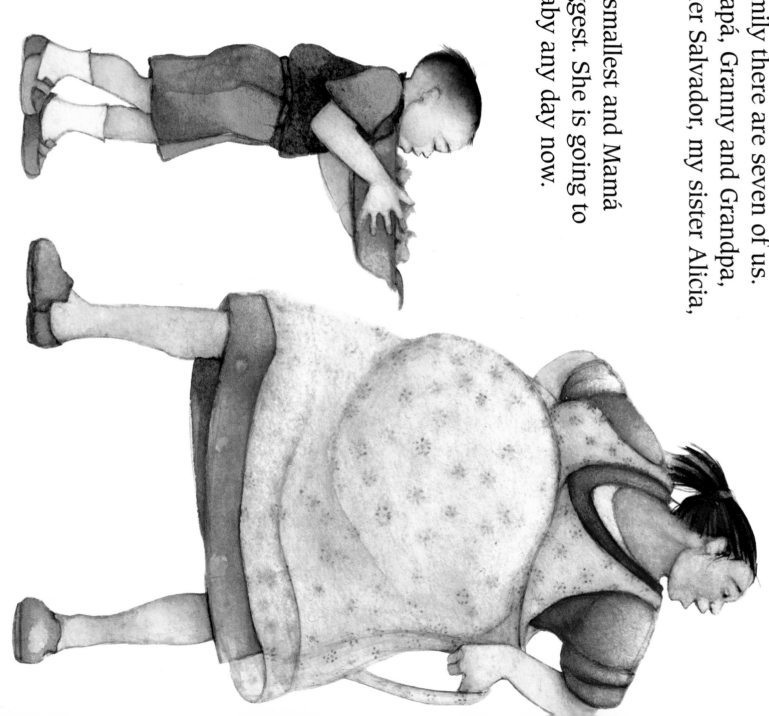

Every day at two o'clock our family eats together in the kitchen, sitting at the big wooden table that Papá made. When we are all at the table Mamá is happy.

Papá is listening to all of us talk at once.

Granny is telling us about the giant tomato growing in the garden.

Grandpa is remembering when he was a young boy.

Salvador is wriggling off his chair to hide under the table between our feet.

And Alicia is asking a thousand questions. I think she is going to be the wisest person in the village.

This Monday Mamá calls from the kitchen, "Antonio, go and tell your father to come and eat. We are having chickpea soup."

I find Papá working in the carpentry shop. He says to me, "I can't come home to eat. I have too much work to do."

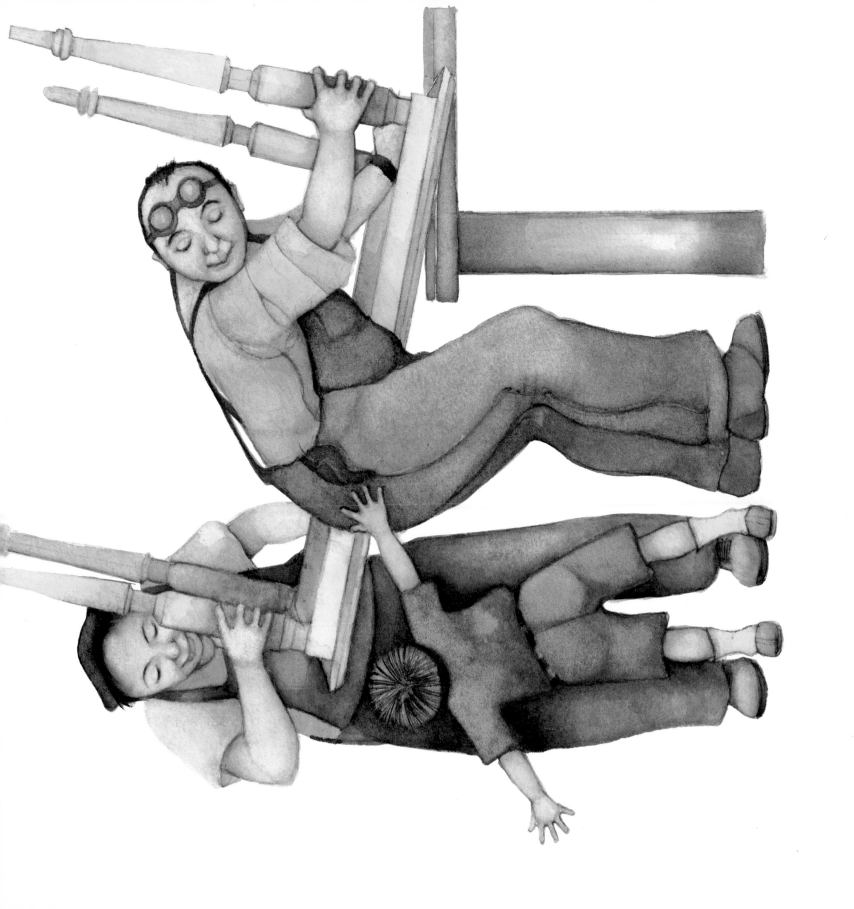

So we have to eat without my father. *"Ay, qué pena! What a pity,"* sighs Mamá.

On Tuesday Mamá calls from the kitchen,
"Antonio, go and tell your sister to come and eat.
Today we are having *empanadas.*"

I find Alicia with her friends, Ana Belén and Cristina.
They are learning to dance the *sevillanas*. Cristina's mother
is clapping to keep the rhythm.

Alicia says, "I can't come home now. I want to
practice dancing because the summer *fiesta*
is starting next week."

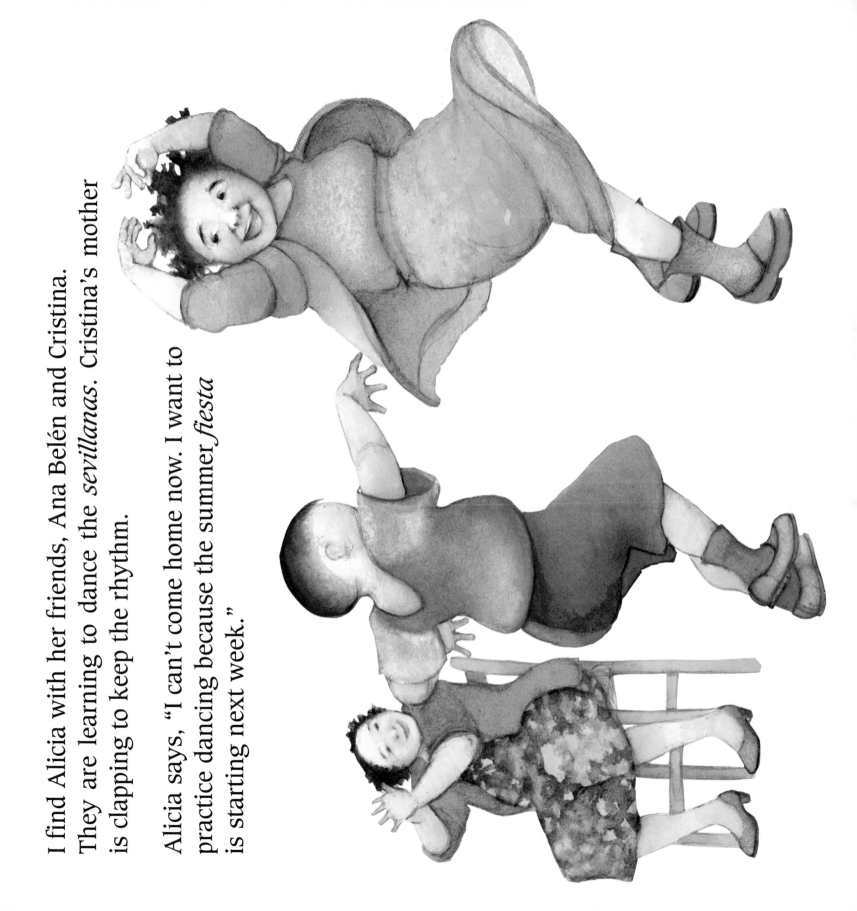

So we have to eat without my sister.
"*Ay, qué pena!*" sighs Mamá.

On Wednesday Mamá calls from the kitchen, "Antonio, go and tell your brother to come and eat. We are having *sardinas*."

I find Salvador playing hide-and-seek in the ruins of the castle with his friends, Luis and Manuel. They are crawling between the fallen old stone blocks.

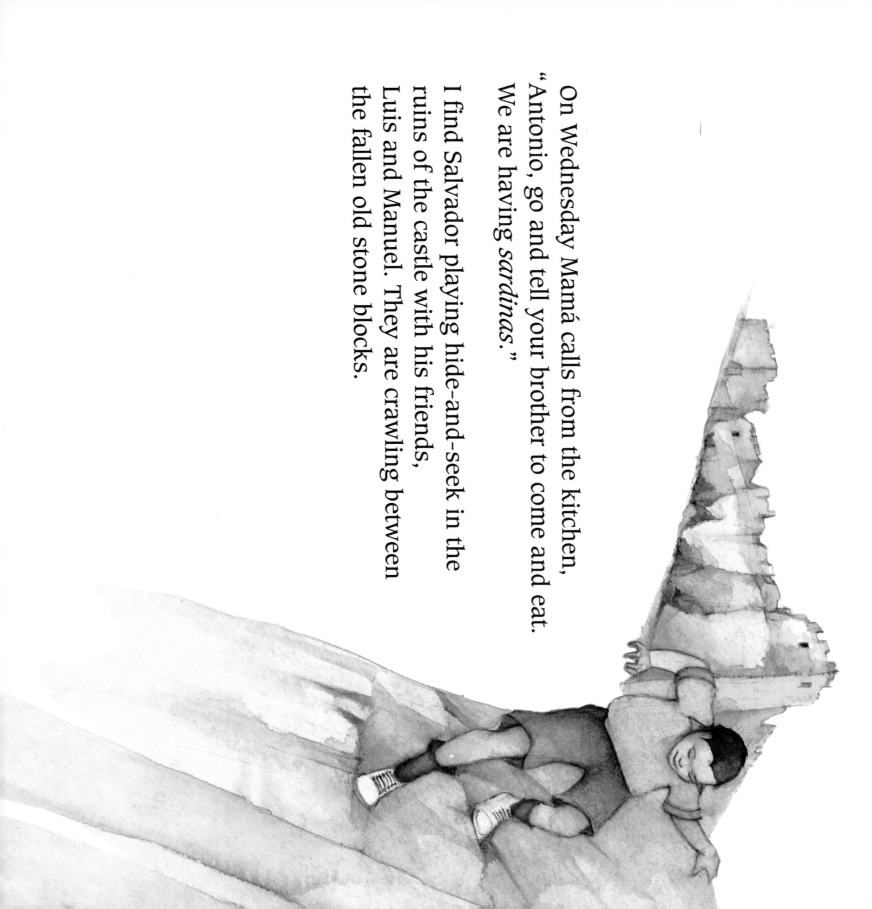

"Shh, tell Mamá I can't come now. I've found the best hiding place in the world!" whispers Salvador.

So we have to eat
without my brother.
"Ay, qué pena!" sighs Mamá.

On Thursday Mamá calls from the kitchen,
"Antonio, go and tell Granny to come and eat.
We are having *gazpacho*."

I find Granny busy in our garden. She says,
"My dear little Antonio, I can't come to the table right now.
I'm busy picking the tomatoes."

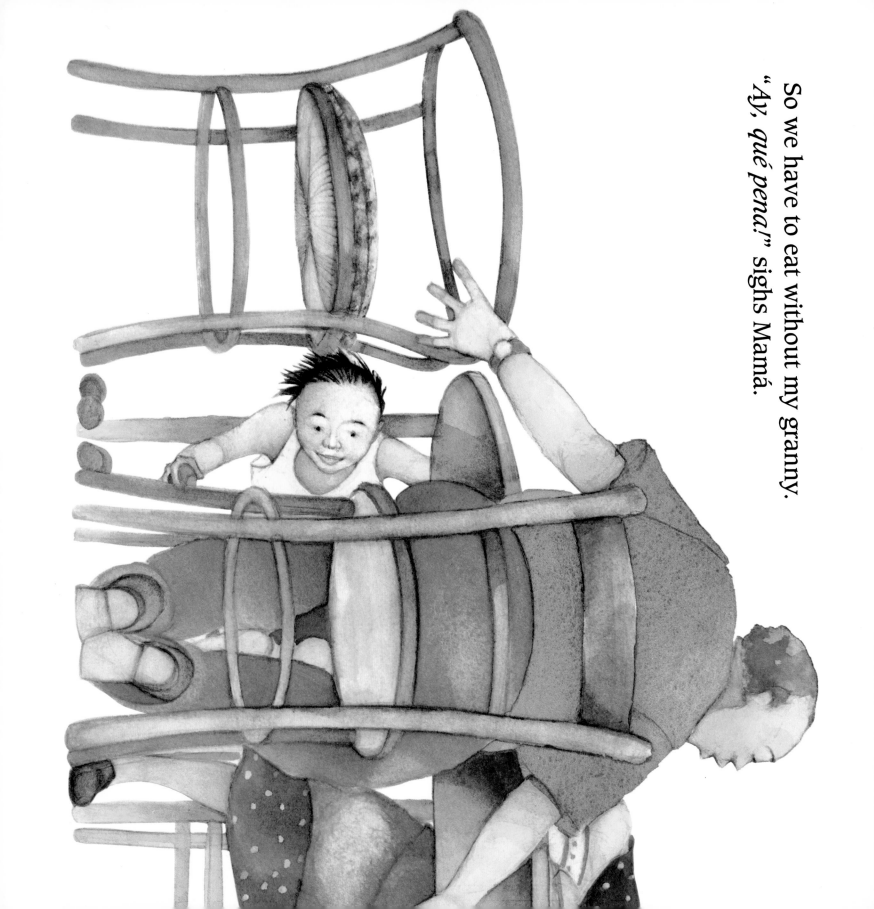

So we have to eat without my granny.

"*Ay, qué pena!*" sighs Mamá.

On Friday Mamá calls from the kitchen, "Antonio, go and tell your grandpa to come and eat. We are having roast *pollo*."

I find Grandpa with his friends in the *cafetería*.
He says, "Little Antonio, I can't come with you right now.
I still have the rest of my story to tell."

So we have to eat without my grandpa.
"Ay, qué pena!" sighs Mamá.

On Saturday we are all sitting at the table ready
to eat—except Mamá. Last night Mamá went to the
hospital to have a baby girl.

I am happy about my new little sister, but I miss Mamá.

"*Ay, qué pena!*" I sigh, just like Mamá! Everyone laughs—and so do I.

On Sunday, one week later, Mamá comes home with little Rosa. We are preparing the prawns, crab, squid, mussels, and saffron rice for the *paella*.

At two o'clock we all sit at the
big wooden table that Papá made.

Papá is making Mamá laugh.
Grandpa is telling us about
when Mamá was a baby.
Granny is planning to grow
a big pumpkin for little Rosa to eat.
Salvador is wriggling off
his chair to hide under
the table, and Alicia is asking
a thousand questions
about babies.

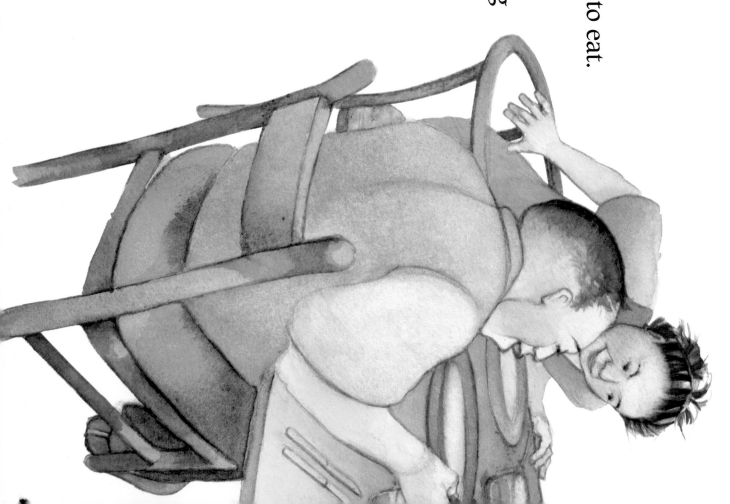

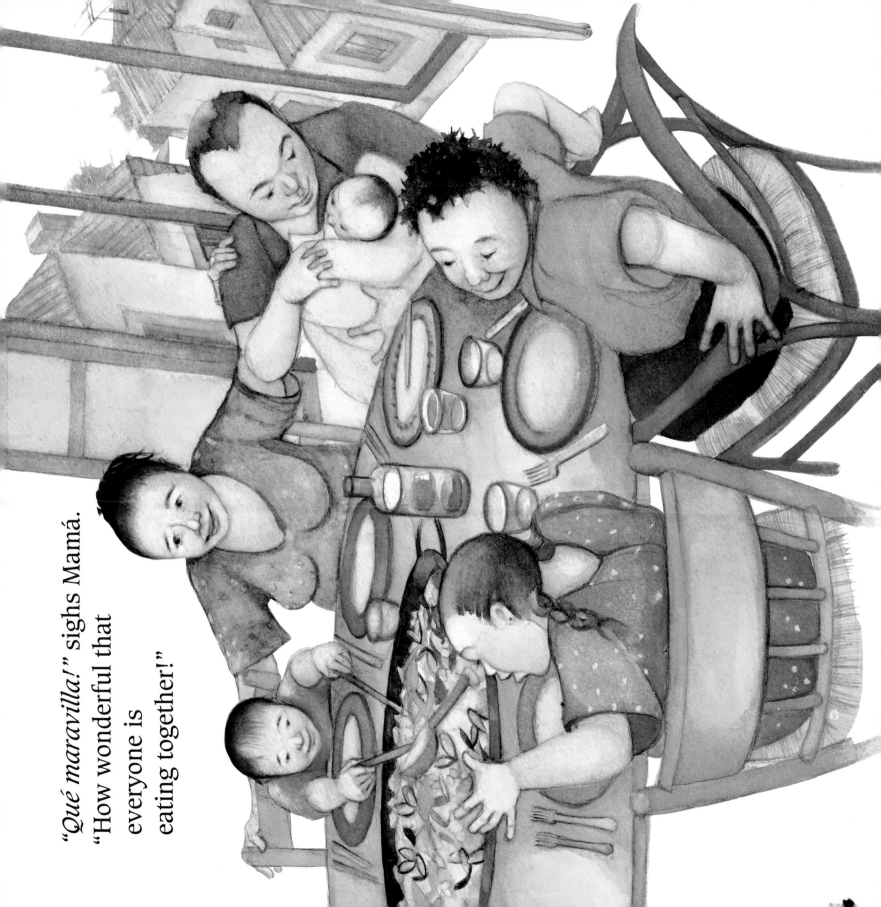

"Qué maravilla!" sighs Mamá. "How wonderful that everyone is eating together!"

Glossary

cafetería — a Spanish café which is a cross between a café and a bar

empanada — a small pie or pastry with a meat or tuna and tomato filling

fiesta — a party or festival

gazpacho — a cold tomato soup from the south of Spain

paella — a rice dish with chicken and seafood

pollo — chicken

qué maravilla — how wonderful

qué pena — what a pity

sardinas — sardines

sevillanas — a type of dance from the south of Spain

For my Spanish Grandma,
abuela Pilar
A.Z.

For *la familia* Vivas
J.V.

Text copyright © 1996 by Ana Zamorano.
Illustrations copyright © 1996 by Julie Vivas.

All rights reserved. Published by Scholastic Inc., by arrangement with Omnibus Books.
Originally published in 1996 by Omnibus Books, a division of the Scholastic Australia Group.

SCHOLASTIC and associated logos are trademarks and/or registered trademarks of Scholastic Inc.

ISBN 0-439-06758-8

12 11 10 9 8 7 6 5 4   3 4/0

Printed in the U.S.A.   08

First Scholastic Trade paperback printing, June 1999

Julie Vivas used watercolor for the illustrations in this book.